SHEILA GREENWALD

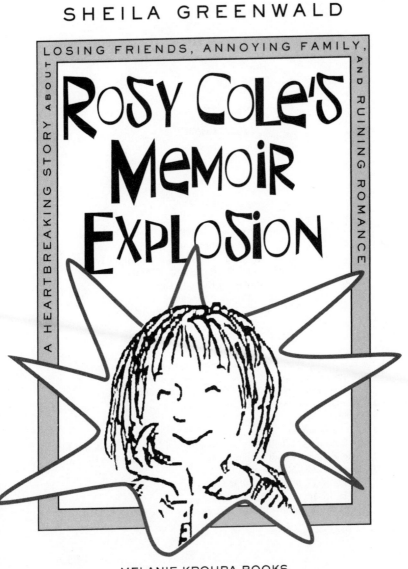

A HEARTBREAKING STORY ABOUT LOSING FRIENDS, ANNOYING FAMILY, AND RUINING ROMANCE

Rosy Cole's Memoir Explosion

MELANIE KROUPA BOOKS
Farrar, Straus and Giroux
New York

For George

Library of Congress Cataloging-in-Publication Data
Greenwald, Sheila.
Rosy Cole's memoir explosion : a heartbreaking story about
losing friends, annoying family, and ruining romance / Sheila
Greenwald.— 1st ed.
p.   cm.
Summary: When Rosy writes a memoir about herself and her
friends for a school assignment, she is surprised when they are
not thrilled with the result.
ISBN-13: 978-0-374-36347-5
ISBN-10: 0-374-36347-1
[1. Authorship—Fiction.   2. Schools—Fiction.]   I. Title.

PZ7.G852Roe 2006
[Fic]—dc22

2004053260

Contents

Rosy Cole's
Memoir
Explosion

A New Dress

My mother burst into my room carrying a big box. "Rosy, dear," she said excitedly, "I just picked up that pink velvet dress you loved from Dream Teen Boutique. The one you said you wanted to wear to Debby's birthday party."

"I'm not going to Debby's birthday party," I told her.

"Why not?" Mom cried in disbelief. "Debby is one of your best friends."

"I wasn't invited," I said.

My mother put the box down on my bed and sat beside it. "What has happened, Rosy?"

I just shook my head. I couldn't speak—and even if I could, I wouldn't have known what to say.

"If you want to talk, I'll be in the kitchen." My mother put her arms around me and kissed my cheek.

After she left, I opened the box. The dress had a pink velvet top with buttons shaped like hearts. The skirt was shiny and soft and full of folds. There was a big sash all around. I slipped it on and looked at myself in the mirror and thought about how, along with no invitation to Debby's birthday party, I had lost all my friends.

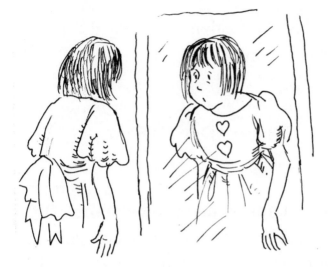

Then I sat down at my desk and picked up my pen. Even though I couldn't talk about it, I could write about it.

1

DYNAMITE!

The minute my teacher, Mrs. Oliphant, wrote the assignment on the board last month, I knew I was in trouble.

Write about the most interesting person in your family.

My name is Rosy Cole. I have a mother and father called Sue and Mike, and two sisters, Anitra and Pippa, who are in college. My Aunt Sylvia and Uncle Charlie sell stationery, Aunt Teddy teaches music, Uncle Ralph is a photographer. Uncle Grover and Aunt Emily are accountants. My cousins are all still in grade school. Even though I love my relatives and they love me, not one of them has been on TV or appeared in *Celebs Galore* or *Lives of the Fab and Famous*. Nobody has ever waited in line for their autographs.

When I got home from school, I told my mother about the assignment.

"Let's take a look in the family albums," she suggested. "Maybe we'll come up with a surprise or two."

Anitra and Pippa squeezed in

around us while Mom turned the pages.

"Just wearing old-fashioned clothes doesn't make them interesting," I yawned.

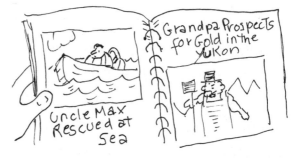

Uncle Max Rescued at Sea

Grandpa Prospects for Gold in the Yukon

"How can you say such a thing?" My mother sounded cross and reached for the two books my Uncle Ralph had written about my sisters. "Ralph was certainly able to make your sisters' lives seem so fascinating that people actually bought the books he wrote about them. There would have been a book about you, too," she reminded me, "if you had let him write it."

I didn't have to look at the books about my sisters. I knew them by heart.

Anitra Dances is full of adorable pictures of Anitra, so happy to study ballet and perform in the *Nutcracker* that every ten-year-old in her right mind would give anything to change places with her.

Pippa Prances shows cute little Pippa riding her horse, Duby, and loving riding so much that any reader who hasn't already signed up for ballet classes would be asking her parents for a horse.

My sisters said Uncle Ralph exaggerated their talents so much that nobody recognized them—including themselves. They said they wished they'd been like me and stopped him before it was too late.

Since I was studying violin with Aunt Teddy, the book Uncle Ralph had wanted to write about me would have been titled *A Very Little Fiddler*. In it he described me as a violin prodigy. The photos he took of me playing the violin were fine.

The photos of my audience were not.

Unfortunately, he never got a shot of the most successful concert I ever gave. It was in Central Park. Everyone applauded my performance and even signed my petition.

Help Me! I have no Talent and should not get lessons, recitals, or encouragement. If you agree, sign my petition.

Of course, I felt bad that I'd let Uncle Ralph down. But good that I'd told the truth about my violin playing.

So now I went to my room and closed the door. Who could I write about? My living relatives were hopeless, and the ones in our family album were no better.

Pippa knocked. "Can I come in?" she asked, coming right in and sitting down. "Cheer up, Rosy," she said. "Nobody has to know if the relative is real. Just make somebody up."

"You mean the way Uncle Ralph did?" I asked.

Pippa nodded. "Sure. There's only one person who really knows about a particular person," she said, "and that's the person herself."

"You mean write about myself and *pretend* to be interesting?" I shook my head. "I don't want to make up things the way Uncle Ralph did."

Pippa put her arm around my shoulder. "You won't have to make things up. You'd be surprised how interesting you are. All you need to do is think about it."

"But the assignment is to write about the most interesting member of my family. If I write about myself, everyone will say I'm conceited."

"No." Pippa shook her head. "Everyone will say you've written a memoir."

"A memoir?"

"At college we have a class that teaches us how to write one, with textbooks and weekly assignments. We read and discuss one another's work in a supportive and nurturing way."

"Supportive and nurturing?"

"No nasty comments," she explained. "Believe me, Rosy, the things that have happened in your life could turn out to be dynamite."

Dynamite! I was so excited by the idea, it never dawned on me to ask who or what she thought might explode.

2

Talent?

Over the weekend, I went to the bookstore to buy the book Pippa said I would need.

By Monday morning, when Mrs. Oliphant went around the room asking everyone who they were going to write about, I was ready.

"The only person I really know about is myself," I informed her. "I want to write a memoir."

"Writing a memoir is not the assignment," Mrs. Oliphant reminded me. She opened the dictionary on her desk and turned to the page for *memoir*. "'A memoir is a narrative from personal experience and memory,'" she read. Then she closed the book. "A memoir is difficult to do. It can be tempting to exaggerate the truth for a better story. That can get you into trouble. It's risky."

The class was so quiet you could practically hear Mrs. Oliphant thinking. "However, I will bend the rules.

If you can be truthful, Rosy, you may write a memoir."

Bend the rules? Difficult? Risky?

Everyone was staring at me as if I were an explorer setting off into unknown territory.

I go to Miss Read's School, which is all girls and private. We wear the same uniform and we live in the same neighborhood. We do the same assignments and we try to get the same good grades. One thing we do *not* do is set off into unknown territory.

I hoped no one could see how my heart was pounding with the thrill of it.

17

At lunch, Hermione Wong plunked down next to me. "How can you write a memoir?" she challenged me. "Nothing's happened to you yet."

"A memoir is about feelings and memories and family and friends," I informed her. "And it just so happens that I have them."

"Well, you're not going to write about me," Hermione shot back. "Because if you do, I want to know exactly what it is you're planning to say."

"Ditto." Christy pulled up a chair on the other side of me and sat down.

"How about the day we all went to the beach with my parents and my cousins?" I asked.

Hermione shook her head. "That day is out."

"But it's *my* memoir. You can't tell me what's in or out."

"That trip to the beach? Are you going to mention how I had a crush on your cousin Eddie?" Hermione was turning pink.

Actually, I didn't know she had a crush on my cousin Eddie.

"Look." Christy leaned over so her face was an inch from mine. "I don't want anything in there about what I said to the lifeguard."

"I don't remember what you said to the lifeguard. I just remember that he told Pippa he thought you were cute."

"He did?" Christy grinned. "Okay. You could put that in. In fact, I would *love* it if you put that in."

"And my cousin Eddie thought you were cute, too," I fibbed to Hermione, who was getting her where-am-I-in-the-picture look.

"Really?" She began to smile.

They were both gazing at me, waiting for more. So I gave them more.

"Actually, Eddie told his brother that he liked your bathing suit," I told Hermione.

She went from pink to glistening. I was on a roll.

"The lifeguard asked Pippa when you were coming back to the beach," I tossed off to Christy, who sucked up so much milk that it came out her nose and she started to choke.

I looked at Hermione and Christy. It was hard to believe they were glistening and choking just because I might include them in my memoir. It dawned

on me that in writing a memoir, I suddenly had a whole lot of *power*.

I bit into my sandwich and chewed
slowly, thinking. "I've changed my mind,"
I said. "I won't use the trip to the
beach. It's boring."

"Boring!" they both yelled at once.

"What will you write, then?" Christy
demanded.

"I don't know yet," I confessed. "But
it says in the how-to-write-a-memoir
book that I need to talk about Talent,
Tears, and Turning Points."

"How about no Talent, but tons of Tears?" Hermione began to laugh. "Like that time you tried to get out of your uncle's book. We all knew you sounded like a dying cat. I couldn't believe you even went to Central Park to collect signatures to support giving up your violin lessons."

"That was *so* terrible," Christy sighed like a soap opera queen. "You must have been humiliated beyond belief."

"Pathetic, too." Linda Dildine pulled up a chair opposite me.

"We didn't know how you got through it," Debby Prusock chimed in.

All my friends at the table were having such a good time feeling sorry for me, they could hardly hide their smiles.

"Why are *you* grinning?" Hermione snapped. "It certainly couldn't have been fun for you."

"It wasn't fun," I agreed.

But it was *exactly* what I needed for my memoir.

RoMaNce

As soon as I got home, I opened *Write Your Life: A How-to Guide for Memoir* and followed the three suggestions for getting started:

1. Meditation: Calm your mind and

open it to the past

2. Tastes, smells, touch, souvenirs, and objects will inspire memory

3. Old photos can help you recall your feelings

Nothing worked.

Page two of *Write Your Life* gave more hints.

EVERY SUCCESSFUL MEMOIR NEEDS
1. Talent, Tears, Turning Points
2. Romantic Relationships
3. Confronting Demons
4. Overcoming Obstacles
5. Family Feuds
6. Rising above Failure
7. A Never-Before-Told Secret (Revealed at the End)
8. Reader Sympathy

Romantic Relationships! At last, maybe I had something.

I picked up the phone and called Christy McCurry's brother, Donald.

Unfortunately, Christy answered. "I'm sick of trying to interview my sister, Dawn," she grumbled. "Maybe I should write a memoir, too."

"It's not easy," I told her. "Along with Talent, Turning Points, and Tears, it needs Family Feuds and Romance."

"Romance," Christy said with a yawn. "I suppose you want to talk to Donald." I heard her yell out, "Pick up the phone, Dodo. Rosy needs Romance."

"You need what?" Donald asked on an extension.

"I'm writing my memoir," I told him in my most dignified tone of voice, grateful he couldn't see the way Christy's words had made me go pink as bubble gum.

"I'm making cocoa."

"Take out a mug for me, I'll be right over." I hung up before he could say no.

Even though he's no talker, I hoped I could persuade Donald to tell me his innermost feelings about our relationship in a way that would make my memoir dynamite.

For years, every time I'd see Christy's older brother, I would feel fizzy as soda water. But he always seemed to be thinking such deep thoughts about great art and world history, he never even looked my way.

Then last spring, I bumped into him at the museum. I was trying to learn how to make myself beautiful from the paintings displayed there. Donald told me I was more fun to be with than any other girl, and that as far as he was concerned, being fun to be with was even more important than being beautiful.

Now, even though Donald isn't exactly my boyfriend, he is a friend and he's definitely a boy and there isn't anybody else who fills that slot . . . So . . .

When I got to Donald's, he was waiting for me. Over his shoulder I could see two mugs of steaming cocoa on the kitchen table. I walked right in and sat down in front of one of them.

Donald watched me open my notebook and take out my pencil, and he smiled the smile that always makes me feel happy and nervous at the same time. "What's up, Rosy?" he asked.

I sipped my cocoa. "I'm writing my memoir," I explained. "I'm telling about a very painful time in my life when my uncle was working on his book about my being a young genius on the violin. It would help if you could reveal your feelings toward me back then."

"I didn't know you then." Donald shrugged. "You were just one of Christy's friends."

"Just *one* of Christy's friends?"

"I mean, you're my friend n-now, Rosy," Donald began to stammer. "But back then, I was only twelve and you were ten. What gives?"

"I need to know your innermost feelings about me."

"I don't talk about stuff like that." He turned his face away. "I'm only thirteen."

"But Romeo was only fifteen."

"Romeo was a character made up for a play." Donald wasn't stammering anymore. He was angry. "I hope you aren't making me into a character for your memoir."

"I'm making you into a person who is important in my *life*. Along with Talent and Tears and Turning Points a memoir needs . . ."

"Needs what?" Donald stormed.

"Rom . . . relationships," I said. Something told me to skip "Romance" for the time being.

"Rosy, I don't have Relationships," he growled. "I have friendships. And as far as I'm concerned, this one is as cold as my cocoa." Donald stood up . . . and then he left.

For a minute, I thought he would come right back and walk me to the

door. When he didn't, I closed my notebook and found my own way out.

In the hall I rang for the elevator. As
I stepped inside, I realized I had set
out in search of a Romantic Relationship and, without even planning on it,
had found Tears instead.

When it came to my memoir, how
lucky was that?

4

A Turning Point?

As I walked in the door, my family was sitting down to an early supper so my sisters could catch their seven o'clock bus back to college.

"Have you found an interesting relative to write about yet?" my father asked me.

"I gave up looking for an interesting relative," I said. "I'm writing a memoir instead."

My mother smiled and tried not to laugh. "But nothing has happened to you yet, Rosy."

"I disagree." Pippa shook her head.

"Even though Uncle Ralph never got one of his phony books out of her, plenty has happened to Rosy."

My mother stopped laughing and looked sad. "Ralph may have exaggerated your talents, but he meant well," she argued. "I hope one day you girls will realize that his books were intended to be loving and kind."

"As far as we could tell, they were intended to make him rich and you proud," Anitra disagreed.

"But don't worry," Pippa added, jumping up from her chair to give my mother a hug. "By writing her memoir, Rosy will overcome her anger and learn to forgive and move on."

"Move on?" Mom asked nervously.

Pippa looked at her watch. "Speaking of moving on, we better get down to the terminal or we'll miss our bus."

After they had gone, my mother came into my room with a photo album of our last holiday trip to the beach. "Rosy, dear," she said softly, "just look at these pictures and you will see proof of the wonderful good times our family has had together."

I opened *Write Your Life: A How-to Guide for Memoir* to page two and the list of what a memoir needs. "Just look at this list," I said, "and you will see that 'Wonderful Good Times' is not on it."

The next morning, I knew something was up the minute I saw Christy and Hermione waiting for me in the lobby.

"We've decided to write memoirs, too," Christy announced. She was practically jumping with excitement. "I'll tell how I am a successful child model and what it's like to be pretty and photogenic and get bookings and go to great places for shoots."

"I'm telling how I won the cello competition at music school," Hermione interrupted. "And how everybody says I have real talent."

"We hope you don't mind our taking your idea," Christy said. "We think you're right. It's much more fun to write about ourselves than someone else."

"It isn't supposed to be fun," I informed Christy. "A memoir has to have Turning Points and Tears and Family Feuds and Romantic Relationships and . . ."

"How do you know all this stuff?" Hermione cut me off before I finished the list.

I took *Write Your Life* out of my knapsack to show them.

Christy flipped the pages. "Can I borrow this?"

"Me first." Hermione grabbed it from her.

"I have a better idea," I said, slowly taking the book back from Hermione and putting it inside my bag.

"What's that?" Hermione asked.

"Watch the bulletin board," I said mysteriously.

Everyone was so curious to know what I was planning that minutes after I posted my notice, there was a small crowd in front of it.

Bulletin Board

Write Your Life
Memoir Workshop
For more info,
watch this
space.

Wednesday morning I posted a sign-up sheet listing the ground rules. Then I added the assignment for our first workshop.

GROUND RULES | FIRST ASSIGNMENT

1. Everyone reads her work
2. Everybody comments
3. Comments MUST BE supportive and kind

Bring a photo of yourself and tell the story behind it.
Sign Up Here

At the end of my last class, when I looked to see how many people were planning to attend, I was amazed. "This is incredible," I said to Hermione. "Five people have already signed up for my workshop."

"What's incredible is that five people have signed up to be supportive and kind," Hermione said, rolling her eyes.

"What's really incredible is that five people have signed up for an experience that could be a turning point in their lives," I informed her.

Hermione didn't say a word. And that was a turning point for sure.

5

More Tears . . .

Wednesday night I read the chapter called "Conducting a Workshop." I wanted to be ready for the next day.

There wasn't enough space in my room for everyone to sit in a circle, so my mother said we could use the living room.

"We will go around the circle so each of us can hold up our photo and tell about it," I began.

"This is me on a shoot," Christy started off. "Here you see how everybody makes a big fuss over me. I am the luckiest girl in the world. I not only have fun—I get paid for it."

"Maybe *I* don't get paid for it," Hermione announced, waving her snapshot in our faces. "But look how everybody is jumping up and down and clapping because I won the cello competition."

"Maybe I'm not that pretty and I don't win music prizes," Debby chimed in, "but my *grades* are the best. Here I am, receiving the math medal for excellence." She beamed and passed the photo to me.

When everybody had finished bragging, there was a pause.

"These are very good," I announced, remembering to be kind and supportive, "but a memoir needs Tears as well as Talent." I held up my list. "It needs Confronting Demons, Overcoming Obstacles, Family Feuds, and Rising above Failure. And then Relationships and Romance and a Never-Before-Told Secret at the end."

"I don't understand." Keisha blinked nervously.

I read from my how-to book. "A memoir needs to be dramatic and interesting."

"How do we do that?" Debby asked.

"Look at your photos again," I advised, "and find the hidden story behind the picture."

Everybody took another look.

"Actually, Mom didn't like my bathing suit," Keisha remembered. "She thought it made me look fat. And diving really scares me. That's an Obstacle." Her face began to pucker. "Do I really want to win swim meets or just impress my parents and friends?"

"This modeling won't last," Christy whimpered. "It's harder and harder to be the prettiest. Soon I'll be washed up and nobody will pay any attention."

"I practice and practice the piano." Linda bit her lip to hold back tears. "I mean, I'm good. But am I good enough? It was all my mom's idea—I'll never measure up to her when she was my age." Linda burst out crying.

"It's awful," Debby admitted. "I have great grades, but every time there's a test, I worry I'll fail." She looked terrible.

Hermione stood up. "I think I'll go back to writing about my cousin Louise."

Suddenly, my entire workshop was heading for the door. "Even though I never went to one before," Keisha said, "this is the *worst* workshop I ever attended."

"But you can't leave now," I pleaded. "We're just getting started. You're on to some very interesting memoirs."

"I'm on to the elevator and out of here," Linda sobbed. "Forget it!"

Forget it!

All my friends wanted was the Talent and Turning Point parts. Not one of them could deal with Tears, Confronting Demons, Overcoming Obstacles, and Family Feuds.

After they were gone, I picked up the photographs they'd left. Was there a story in every picture just like the book said?

If there was, I could see it was up to me, Rosy Cole, to find it. And to write not just my own memoir but *theirs* as well.

6

CONFRONTING DEMONS

On Monday, when everybody handed in the assignment, I asked Mrs. Oliphant for more time. "I'm not just writing about myself, but my generation," I explained.

"*Your* generation?" Hermione Big-Ears hollered.

When I didn't answer, I heard her mutter, "What do you know about it?"

"Not as much as I'd like," I said. "It would really help if my friends would give me interviews."

"Interviews?" Linda asked. "You mean like on the morning TV shows?"

"The same," I nodded, as if I had the idea before she mentioned it.

She clapped her hands excitedly. "Could I be the very first?"

"How about this afternoon?" I suggested.

"Don't be a simp," Hermione warned Linda. "Rosy will just make you look like a loser."

But Linda wasn't listening.

As soon as school was out, I ran home to set up.

When Linda arrived, she was carrying two big shopping bags. "I'm so thrilled about this," she gushed. "I came prepared."

I was prepared, too. I had saved notes and photos from the workshop, and Dad let me borrow his video camera. "So you feel you can never measure up to your mother?"

"In many ways, she can't measure up to me," Linda disagreed, reaching into one of the shopping bags. "Mom can't do appliqué and macramé the way I can." She held up a sample of her work. "I learned this at craft camp."

"What would you say is an Obstacle you face?" I asked, eyeing the macramé.

"How to market this stuff," Linda confided. "I have a closetful. You can order by calling me at home or through the mail."

She looked straight into the camera

and held up a large cardboard sign that showed her address and phone number. "Five dollars an item," she shouted. "Shipping and handling not included."

I stopped filming. "This is supposed to be an interview, Linda," I reminded her. "Not a sales pitch."

"What's the difference?" She began packing up her shopping bags.

The next morning, after Linda reported to everybody at school about her "interview," I had three more requests.

Hermione was looking to sell her collection of old trading cards. She gave me a price list and photos. Christy said there was a hole in her modeling schedule for spring and to "tell everybody out there I'm available." She gave me the name of her agent.

"What's going on here?" I asked Debby, who was trying to unload some fudge she made last year at Christmas. Two fifty a box.

"You said celebrity interviews like on the morning TV shows," she explained. "We wanted to help you out even if we don't have movies, books, plays, or restaurants to pitch."

My friends were hiding their true stories behind sales pitches. It was obvious now that I would have to write our memoir without their help.

I turned to my trusty guidebook for inspiration. This time, my friends' photos told me all I wanted to know. I

could see the story behind every single
one of them.

If I looked hard enough,
I could even see Tears

and Demons
to Confront

and Rising above Failure.

I was glad I had notes. I gave each friend a full page, which included everything they'd blurted out at my workshop, including Keisha Wilson's worrying about looking fat in a bathing suit and Debby's fear of failing.

I added five pages about myself. I wanted to tell the truth, but I was sure readers would understand that to make a better story I needed to exaggerate a little.

Even though I still didn't have Over-coming Obstacles, Family Feuds, Rising above Failure, and a Never-Before-Told Secret, there were enough items on my list to make ten pages.

I was able to finish writing part one of my memoir in only two days. I made ten copies on my dad's Xerox machine and put them in separate envelopes.

Then, on the last day of school before vacation, I handed in my memoir to Mrs. Oliphant with a note explaining that I would submit part two after vacation.

"I'll read this over the holiday," she promised.

At our class party we sang songs for Christmas and Hanukkah and Kwanzaa. Then Mrs. Oliphant dismissed us early because heavy snow had begun to fall.

All the way home we were still singing. There were holiday decorations and lights up and down Madison Avenue. Shops were full of people and music. The snow made everything soft, like a scene in a movie that might have been based on a book . . . maybe a memoir . . . maybe even mine.

Christy had a camera, so we asked a sidewalk Santa to take our photo, and Christy promised she'd send us each a souvenir copy to remember the day. Suddenly, it dawned on me that I might have another use for the picture.

The Author and Her Friends

BEST SELLER ←

"Don't forget my birthday lunch Sunday at the Noodle Shop on Lex," Christy reminded us.

"Who's invited?" Hermione asked.

"Debby and Keisha and Linda and you." Christy counted on her fingers. "My folks, my sister"—she paused—"Rosy, and Donald."

Donald!

How perfect could it get?

7

OVERCOMING OBSTACLES

Saturday was busy. My sisters came home from college. I didn't say a word about the memoir. It would be a wonderful surprise for them. It would be a surprise for Christy and my classmates, too.

My gift to Christy was not going to be the usual cheap-jewelry-perfume-beauty-care junk, but something timeless to enrich her inner life. *My Life and Times, the Story of the Newest Generation: Part One* didn't need fancy paper wrapping. So at the stationery store I bought a shiny purple plastic envelope and put my memoir inside. I attached a sticker in the shape of a star.

Sunday morning I dressed for the party. Since I wanted to look like a real writer, I borrowed Pippa's black turtleneck, Dad's beret, and Anitra's glasses.

Except for the not-seeing part, it was perfect.

By the time I arrived at the Noodle Shop on Lex, everybody was there.

I put Christy's gift at the bottom of the pile of presents beside a goody bag full of party poppers, whistles, and funny hats.

"What took you so long?" Hermione asked, glaring at my gift for Christy. "It certainly wasn't special wrapping."

"Fancy paper is a waste of time and money," I heard Donald mutter under his breath.

Was he defending me? I tried to catch his eye, but, as usual, he looked away. His ears, however, were red.

"It's the thought that counts," he said. He *was* defending me! And after he found out what was inside the purple envelope, I knew he would be proud of me, the voice of the newest generation—*our* generation!

The party went on forever, but I was too excited to eat a single dumpling. Finally, just when I thought she would never get around to it, Christy began to open her presents.

There was a DVD from Debby, a bottle of perfume from Linda, a scarf from Keisha, and a wallet made of glow-in-the-dark plastic from Hermione. Each present was passed around the table for everyone to say ooh and aah.

When she got to my envelope, Christy shook it. "Ice skates?" she joked.

"It's a special gift to you," I said, "and to all my friends. It's the story of us."

I stood up, opened my copy, and began to read to them. *"My Life and Times, the Story of the Newest Generation: Part One."*

I explained that my being grounded for weeks, being forced to practice the violin while locked in my room with no supper, made it possible for me to understand all of them better than they understood themselves.

Except for some gasps when I described waterlogged Keisha in her too-tight suit, Linda warping the piano

keys with tears, Debby grubbing for grades, Hermione chained to her cello, and Christy hysterical over the zits that would ruin her career, the room was so quiet I could have heard a chopstick drop.

"This memoir is for all of us," I concluded. "For me and Christy and Debby and Keisha and Linda and Hermione. For all my friends who couldn't tell your own stories, I have done it for you."

I folded my papers and looked out at my audience to see just how much my words had moved them.

Debby stood up. "We never asked you to tell our stories," she growled. "And nobody ever grounded you or took away your dinner."

"You just exaggerated the stuff we told you so you could make your story dramatic and yourself important." Hermione shook her finger at me.

The only ones who weren't glaring were Christy's parents, her sister, and

Donald. They looked puzzled and a little sad.

I was so stunned I couldn't move. My heart began banging and my eyes stung and I knew any minute they would start spouting tears. I picked up my jacket and stumbled toward the door. Donald followed me and pulled at my elbow. Was he going to come to my rescue?

"You forgot your fortune cookie," he said, putting something in my hand. It wasn't a fortune cookie though.

It was a napkin. On it Donald had written:

Use friends?

Was *he* angry, too? How could it be that he didn't understand? How could it be that *nobody*, not one of them, understood? Why weren't they proud of me for being brave enough to tell the truth about all of our lives?

I could see my friends putting on funny hats and starting to pull the strings on their party poppers. No one even looked my way. I guess my memoir had been the biggest popper on the table. Pippa had warned me memoirs could be dynamite. And sure enough, it felt as if this one had just exploded in my face.

All the way home, I told myself that my friends would be sorry for rejecting me. Probably by the time I opened my front door, they would be calling to apologize.

But when I opened the door, the apartment was silent. I crossed out Overcoming Obstacles on my list. At this rate, part two of my memoir would take no time at all.

After that, I sat on my bed and checked to see if the phone was broken. Then I waited for it to ring.

While I waited, I began thinking somebody should invent a phone that rings when you want it to. I lay down on my bed and thought while they were at it they should invent a pillow that is also a sponge.

8

FAMILY FEUDS

During the vacation, I had even more time than I'd expected for thinking about my future.

I don't know how my family guessed that something was wrong, but they did.

Even though my parents and my sisters were busy wrapping gifts and preparing for our family's holiday party, they kept asking me if I was okay.

It seemed that they were the only people who still cared. To show my gratitude, I presented each of them with a copy of my memoir.

Pippa and Anitra had just finished reading it when Uncle Ralph and Aunt Teddy arrived for dinner.

"And what have you been up to, Rosy?" Uncle Ralph asked.

"I've written my memoir," I said.

"Your *memoir*?" Aunt Teddy hooted, and then she and Uncle Ralph burst into gales of laughter.

"She's hardly lived," Uncle Ralph sputtered.

"She has lived long enough to tell the world how damaged she was by *A Very Little Fiddler*," Pippa argued. "All Rosy needs is a few more scenes to make the story complete."

"I agree," Anitra nodded. "She forgot to describe how it was *me* who gave her the idea to perform in Central Park."

"*You?*" Pippa cried. "I was the one who advised her to do that. I was the one who suggested the petition. You weren't even home."

Anitra glared down the table in my direction. "Of course I was home. *Tell* her, Rosy," she demanded.

How could they both think everything that happened to me was about *them*, when I was the one suffering? I could hardly stand it. My eyes blurred and a tear rolled down my face.

"Excuse me." My mother tapped her glass for attention. "Can we have a little consideration for the sake of family peace?"

"Family peace and consideration," Uncle Ralph roared, "do not sell memoirs."

"Sell memoirs?" I gasped. Did Uncle Ralph think my best-seller dream could come true?

"I was on the wrong track with the book I did about you, Rosy," he said excitedly. "But your memoir . . . I can see it now: *A Driven Child.*"

"Spare us," my mother pleaded.

But it was too late. Uncle Ralph followed me into my room as soon as dinner was over to look at what I had written.

"I see," he said, flipping my pages and getting even more excited. "You used the pictures I took to tell your story in your own way. This time, we just might have a winner."

He shook my hand to congratulate me before we joined the family.

"Don't worry, Sis," Uncle Ralph tried to reassure my mother. "Rosy won't let me down. This story won't backfire like the one I wrote. This time, it will be in her own words."

"I wish I'd had a book in *my* words," Pippa glowered at Uncle Ralph.

"Ditto," Anitra agreed.

"Your words!" I couldn't help saying. "You didn't even get the facts straight about what happened to me!"

Now Pippa and Anitra both glowered at *me*.

Uncle Ralph patted Mom on the back. "Rosy will come through this time. Wait and see." Then he grinned from ear to ear. "Why don't you write a memoir, too, Sis?" he said. "Call it *How I Survived Three Daughters*."

"You can't do that, Mom," Pippa yelped. "We've told you all our private stuff."

My mother shook her head. "Of course not," she said wearily. "Trust and privacy is what makes us a family."

"But betraying trust and privacy is what makes a hot story," Uncle Ralph said. "You can't have it both ways."

For a moment everybody was silent. Then Aunt Teddy looked at her watch. "Isn't it time to take the annual holiday photo?" she asked.

We all sat together on the couch. "Everybody smile," Aunt Teddy said.

We did our best.

Everybody thought the family party had been a flop. But when I checked my list, I could see that for me it was actually a huge success.

I wondered just how much more success I could stand.

9

Rising above Failure

The first morning after vacation, things did not go well. Hermione and Christy were not waiting for me in the lobby like they usually did. In school, everybody was talking about what they had done over the holiday. Everyone but me. And at lunch, there were empty chairs on either side

of mine. What else could go wrong?

After lunch, Mrs. Oliphant handed back my memoir.

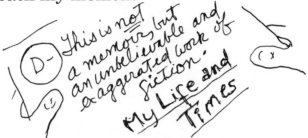

That did it! Suddenly I wasn't upset—I was *mad*. Didn't Mrs. Oliphant know that any memoir needs a little exaggeration to make it interesting? Just wait till she saw my book number-one on the best-seller list. Then she'd brag to her friends that I was one of her students. Wait till Hermione, Christy, Linda, and the others heard. They would be fighting over the chair next to mine in the lunchroom and elbowing for a spot on the sidewalk when I walked home from school. They'd be happy if I agreed to forgive them.

In the meantime, I walked home from school by myself.

The phone was ringing as I came in the door. It was Uncle Ralph.

"Exciting news, Rosy," he said. "*Tell All* magazine is thinking of starting a section for preteens willing to confide their troubles. If you could manage to come up with five more pages about yourself, they will consider publishing your work."

"*Tell All*?" To appear in *Tell All* could mean I would be a certified celebrity like the ones in *Lives of the Fab and Famous* and *Celebs Galore*. It was the seal of approval for "interesting." I could just imagine the headlines and everyone's reaction.

"They want raw truth," Uncle Ralph warned. "You could be very unpopular."

"I already am."

"I'll pick up your new pages Friday afternoon at five," Uncle Ralph told me. "That way, I can go over them before I deliver them to the magazine next week."

"Five o'clock. I'll be ready," I promised. "This time, I won't let you down."

I took off my jacket and started counting the words in my memoir. I already had ten pages with fifty words on each page. That made five hundred. Now I needed another five pages, or two hundred and fifty words. Most of all, I needed Rising above Failure and a Never-Before-Told Secret. The first was easy. I would Rise above Failure with the publication of my memoir in *Tell All* magazine. But a Never-Before-Told Secret?

The next morning, when I caught up with Christy and Hermione, they pretended to pull zippers across their mouths and button them for good measure.

"To be continued," Christy hissed between zippers and buttons without looking at me. "I don't want to say anything that's going into somebody's memoir."

"I'm not somebody," I said. "I'm Rosy Cole, author of *My Life and Times, the Story of the Newest Generation: Part One*, which will soon be published in *Tell All* magazine."

Christy gasped. Then she clapped her hands in delight. "Well, since you'll be so famous, everyone will definitely want to read your friends' stories— about you. We could fill an entire issue with *The Real Rosy Cole Story*."

I tried to swallow, but my throat was suddenly dry. "What will you say?"

"Oh, there's *so* much," Christy crooned. "How about the time you lost your costume for the Dancing Fairy?"

"And borrowed Linda's size-two tights because you said they were a perfect fit," Hermione went on.

"Until they split down the middle." Christy was laughing so hard she had to stop walking. "Remember that red rash Rosy came down with just before the math final?" she asked Hermione.

"You mean the one that came off on Mrs. Oliphant's hand when she touched Rosy's forehead to see if she had a fever?"

"Oh, stop," I cried. "I was much younger then."

"And there was the anonymous love note she sent Donald," Christy whispered to Hermione.

"You never got the whole story," I interrupted her.

"I got a good story," Christy said. "And that's what counts."

She and Hermione burst out laughing and broke into a run.

In school, all I could think about was how my friends were writing lies about me. I tried to cheer myself up. At least I could put this new misery to good use.

At home, I sat down to write. All I got out of it was another fifty words.

I was still two hundred short. I'd already included how my parents pushed me and my uncle used me and my friends were jealous of me and Donald was angry with me. What else could I say? And what about a Never-Before-Told Secret?

I made a list of all the ways I could try to find more heartbreak and disappointment. But the next day in school, when Linda asked me what I was wearing to Debby's birthday party, I realized I already had as much as I needed.

"Didn't you get an invitation?" She put her hand over her mouth, like she'd made a big mistake.

"I haven't checked the mail yet," I said.

"Debby's brother's band will play," Linda gushed. "And Debby's mom is paying Donald McCurry to do portraits of everybody as a party favor."

When I got home, the mailbox was empty.

I called Hermione. "I hear Debby's having a birthday party."

"It's a small thing. She's not asking the whole class, just a few close friends."

"I thought I was a close friend."

"Close friends don't blab about you in their memoirs just to make themselves famous." Hermione took a deep breath. "I'm sorry, Rosy," she said. But she didn't sound sorry at all.

By the end of the week, everybody was discussing what they would write about me for *The Real Rosy Cole Story* and what they would wear to Debby's birthday party on Saturday.

"I'm having a sleepover tonight and

my mom's got a great video," Keisha announced. Then she read off a list of who would be invited. When I didn't hear my name, I wondered if there was another list.

I was surely on that one.

As soon as school was out, everybody headed off for a slice at Vinnie's. When I came in the door, nobody made room at the table for me. I sat by myself and watched while they passed around a notebook with a cover that said *The Real Rosy Cole Story*.

When everybody got up to leave, no one even waved goodbye.

I asked Vinnie to wrap up my slice so I could take it home.

"All of a sudden you can't eat?" Vinnie looked worried. "You got a food problem?"

"No appetite," I said. "Maybe later." I shook my head. A food problem, me? But then I remembered how I couldn't eat a single dumpling at Christy's birthday party. Maybe I *did* have a food problem! Had I lost my appetite without even knowing it? Had I kept it a secret even from myself?

"Hey," Vinnie said, reaching back for a box. He slipped a whole small pizza with extra cheese into it. "For later. Warm it up, maybe you'll eat." Then he winked. "It's our little secret."

Secret? I smiled. "Don't worry about me, Vinnie," I said, taking the box. He was surprised when I put fifty cents in the tip jar. I couldn't thank him enough.

I ran all the way home. I could hardly wait to start writing about my eating disorder.

But before I had even finished two lines, I got a little carried away.

As I put the empty box and wrappers in the trash, I knew it wasn't true that I couldn't eat. It wasn't true that my family punished me for not practicing. It wasn't true that my friends were nervous wrecks.

But it *was* true that to make my memoir a success I had written a lot of baloney.

After a while, my mother came home from work. She was carrying a box from the Dream Teen Boutique. When I couldn't find the words to explain to her why I wasn't invited to Debby's party, she kissed me and left me alone.

I picked up my pen again, and this time, without even trying, the words that were deep inside me flowed onto my paper.

The hours flew by, because when my mother knocked on my door to announce "Uncle Ralph is here to pick up your pages," I was still writing.

"I see you've been working," Uncle Ralph said with a big smile.

Before I could explain, he scooped up the papers and sat down on my bed to read what I had written.

When he was done, he stared at the rug for a moment and then cleared his throat. *"Why I Was Not Invited to Debby Prusock's Party* is not a memoir for *Tell All* magazine, Rosy."

"No, it isn't," I agreed.

"Even though it's very moving in its own way." Uncle Ralph took out a big handkerchief and blew his nose. His eyes were red around the edges. "I'm so sorry for you."

He wasn't the only one. Suddenly *I*

was so sorry for me that I could hardly stand it. "First it was *A Very Little Fiddler*," I began to blubber, "and now this. I have disappointed you twice. I haven't even got a Never-Before-Told Secret, and Overcoming Obstacles would take a miracle."

Uncle Ralph hugged me and passed back the rumpled pages. "Who knows, kiddo, maybe the miracle is right in your hands."

10

The Secret . . . at Last!

Saturday afternoon I took a bath, and put on the dress from Dream Teen.

"Where are you going?" my mother asked when she saw me zip up my jacket.

"To finally Confront My Demons and Overcome My Obstacles," I said.

Outside Debby's door I could hear laughter and the band tuning up.

Debby was surprised to see me. Just behind her I could see balloons and a big banner.

"Happy birthday," I told Debby. "This is for you and all my friends." I handed her a copy of *Why I Wasn't Invited to Debby Prusock's Party*.

"We know why you weren't in-vited to Debby's party," Hermione said crisply. "You don't have to tell us." She grabbed the manuscript and held up the pages as if they were dead rats.

Debby took the pages back from her and began to read: "This is the true story about how in no time flat I wrote a memoir that began with the truth, but wound up telling whoppers about myself, my family, and my friends."

While Debby read, I checked to see if I was detonating another explosion. Once again, just like in the Noodle Shop, everybody was quiet.

Suddenly, Linda sighed. "Oh, this is good," she said. "It's so sad." She put her arm around me and gave me a hug.

"Reader Sympathy," I said, nodding, and everyone laughed.

Donald opened his sketchbook. "By the way, that's a nice dress. You could be my first portrait."

I tried to sit perfectly still.

Hermione put a glass of raspberry punch in my hand. "It's too bad you worked so hard on that memoir and it was all for nothing," she said.

All for nothing?

Was that true?

Did I really have a memoir explosion all for nothing?

Suddenly I couldn't help smiling.

"Why are you grinning?" Hermione asked suspiciously.

"Please hold still," Donald said, so I couldn't open my mouth to tell them why I was grinning. And then I had another idea: I *wouldn't* tell them—not yet. Which would make this a great secret. In fact, a Never-Before-Told Secret . . .

Could it be that my memoir exploding days were not over yet?